Words to Know Befor

boarded

eventually

excited

marbles

microphone

peered

quiet

substitute

wondered

www.rourkeeducationalmedia.com

Edited by Precious McKenzie
Illustrated by Helen Poole
Art Direction and Page Layout by Renee Brady

Library of Congress PCN Data

Who's Mr. Goldfluss? / Colleen Hord
ISBN 978-1-61810-185-3 (hard cover) (alk. paper)
ISBN 978-1-61810-318-5 (soft cover)
Library of Congress Control Number: 2012936786

Rourke Educational Media
Printed in China, Artwood Press Limited,
  Shenzhen, China

rourkeeducationalmedia.com

customerservice@rourkeeducationalmedia.com • PO Box 643328 Vero Beach, Florida 32964

Who's Mr. Goldfluss?

By Colleen Hord

Illustrated by Helen Poole

As the children boarded the Safe Harbor school bus, they all wondered who the new bus driver was.

When the children were seated, the driver announced, "My name is Mr. Goldfluss. I am your substitute driver for a few days."

DRIVER:
Mr. Goldfluss

"It is my job to get you home safely, so please follow these rules." Mr. Goldfluss held up a large poster.

He read the rules over the bus microphone.

1. ~~ALWAYS~~ stay in your seats.

2. ~~ALWAYS~~ use quiet voices.

3. ~~ALWAYS~~ keep your feet out of the aisle.

4. ~~ALWAYS~~ keep the windows closed.

5. When we get to the railroad tracks, everyone must be quiet-~~ALWAYS~~.

6. ~~ALWAYS~~ wait until the bus stops before you get up to leave.

The children all looked at each other. "Who is this Mr.Goldfluss? He has too many rules!"

"Our old bus driver was more fun!"

As the bus pulled out of the school parking lot, the wind started to blow, and hail, the size of marbles, started falling from the sky. It was hard for Mr. Goldfluss to see the road.

The children were very excited. They jumped out of their seats and opened the windows to watch the storm.

Mr. Goldfluss calmly reminded them of the rules and asked everyone to return to their seats. The children grumbled and whined as they closed the windows.

1. ~~ALWAYS~~ stay in your seats.

2. ~~ALWAYS~~ use quiet voices.

3. ~~ALWAYS~~ keep your feet out of the aisle.

4. ~~ALWAYS~~ keep the windows closed.

5. When we get to the railroad tracks, everyone must be quiet— ~~ALWAYS~~.

6. ~~ALWAYS~~ wait until the bus stops before you get up to leave.

Eventually, the children quieted down and peered out the windows. They all thought Mr. Goldfluss was too strict.

The children watched the trees bending from the fierce wind and the cars crashing into each other as they slid on the slippery road.

The hailstones slammed against the bus windows so hard the children were afraid the glass would shatter.

Mr. Goldfluss pulled the bus over to the curb.

The children looked to the front of the bus. They all wondered why he was stopping the bus.

"We are going to stay parked here until the storm passes," said Mr. Goldfluss. "Once the storm passes, it will be safe to drive again."

The children didn't want to wait. They wanted to get home fast so they could play. But they listened to Mr. Goldfluss.

"Thank you for following the rules," said Mr.Goldfluss. "It is hard to drive in a storm, but when you follow the rules, you are helping me do my job."

The children all smiled at Mr. Goldfluss.
Now they all knew who he was.
Mr. Goldfluss was someone who helped
them stay safe.

After Reading Activities

You and the Story...

Have you ever been in a storm? Describe how you felt.

If you were a bus driver and you were driving in a storm, what would you do?

What do you think the bus rules should be?

Words You Know Now...

Read the list of words. Can you find the verbs? What does the –ed on the end of a verb mean?

boarded   peered
eventually   quiet
excited   substitute
marbles   wondered
microphone

You Could...Let Community Helpers Know You Are Thankful For Them

- Draw a picture showing how bus drivers keep students safe.

- Make a thank you card for the bus drivers or playground helpers at your school. Thank them for keeping you safe.

- Write a different story about a substitute bus driver, or other community helper, who keeps you safe.

About the Author

Colleen Hord is an elementary teacher. Her favorite part of her teaching day is Writer's Workshop. She enjoys kayaking, camping, walking on the beach, and reading in her hammock.

Ask The Author!
www.rem4students.com

About the Illustrator

Helen Poole lives in Liverpool, England, with her fiancé. Over the past ten years she has worked as a designer and illustrator on books, toys, and games for many stores and publishers worldwide. Her favorite part of illustrating is character development. She loves creating fun, whimsical worlds with bright, vibrant colors. She gets her inspiration from everyday life and has her sketchbook with her at all times as inspiration often strikes in the unlikeliest of places!